MISSION ALERT

GREYFIELDS

Bloomsbury Education
An imprint of Bloomsbury Publishing Plc

50 Bedford Square
London
WC1B 3DP
UK

1385 Broadway
New York
NY 10018
USA

www.bloomsbury.com

BLOOMSBURY and the Diana logo are trademarks of Bloomsbury Publishing Plc

First published in 2017 by Bloomsbury Education

ISBN   PB: 978-1-4729-2968-6
ePub: 978-1-4729-2969-3
ePDF: 978-1-4729-2970-9

2 4 6 8 10 9 7 5 3 1

Printed and bound in China by Leo Paper Products

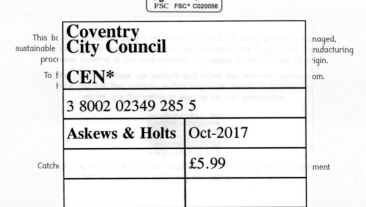

MISSION ALERT
GREYFIELDS

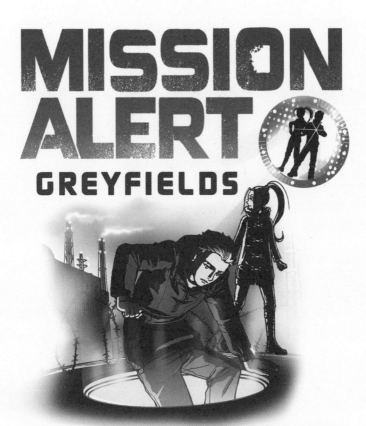

BENJAMIN HULME-CROSS

Illustrated by
Kanako and Yuzuru

BLOOMSBURY EDUCATION
AN IMPRINT OF BLOOMSBURY

LONDON OXFORD NEW YORK NEW DELHI SYDNEY

Tom and his twin sister Zilla go to a boarding school. They don't like it very much. But Tom and Zilla have a secret. They work as spies for the Secret Service. Sometimes there is a spy mission that children are better at than grown-ups. That's when Tom and Zilla get their next Mission Alert!

CONTENTS

Chapter One

Tom and Zilla were playing cards. It was the beginning of half term. All the other kids had gone home but Tom and Zilla were staying at school like they always did.

They had both been looking forward to spending lots of time outside. But it was pouring with rain and they were stuck indoors. "I'm so bored!" said Tom.

Just then, both of their special watches started vibrating. That could mean only one thing. Tom put his watch on speaker.

"Agents, here is your next mission!" said Marcus, their handler at Mission Control.

"Listen carefully. This mission affects everyone in the country. You must succeed. It's a matter of life and death!"

Tom and Zilla looked at each other. This mission sounded even more important than usual.

"I am sure you are aware of the Greyfields Power Station," said Marcus.

Tom nodded. Greyfields was a brand new nuclear power station. It was going to be switched on later that week.

"Some protesters are camping next to the power station," said Marcus.

"So what?" asked Zilla. "It's OK for people to protest if they don't like nuclear energy."

"You're right," said Marcus. "But we think that the protesters will try to stop the power station from working and that could cause a nuclear disaster. There is one protester who we are really worried about. Your mission will be to get close to her. Find out what she is planning. Stop her if you can."

"So why don't you just arrest her?" Zilla asked.

"The protesters have got very good at spotting our spies," Marcus replied. "The last one we sent in was discovered within twenty-four hours. We need to use agents the protesters would never suspect – and that means you. Now, take a look at this map of Greyfields."

A map of the power station came up on the watch screens. Tom and Zilla studied it well. They had been trained to be able to remember maps.

"Now look at this photo," said Marcus. "This is the protester we want you to follow."

A profile came up on screen.

Name: Ana Markova

Age: 28

Background: Grew up in Moscow. Now a student living in London. Known to have broken into nuclear power stations before.

Chapter 2

A taxi dropped Tom and Zilla just down the road from the gates of Greyfields. They paid the driver and put on their rucksacks.

The rucksacks were heavy with tents and sleeping bags, and all the other things they had been given for the mission.

"I don't agree with nuclear power," said Zilla. "What if there is an accident and nuclear fuel leaks out? We could all die."

"That's why we have to stop this woman," said Tom. "It sounds like she wants to cause a nuclear leak!"

They walked towards a group of protesters who were standing outside Greyfields in the rain. When they joined the rest of the group, Zilla reached into her bag and pulled out a flag made out of a sheet. It said NO TO NUCLEAR in thick felt tip.

Zilla and Tom started waving the flag around. There was a man in a red coat standing at the front of the protesters, shouting at them through a megaphone.

"The nuclear waste from this power station will go into the sea. We are all in danger!" shouted the man in the red coat.

"WE DEMAND A NUCLEAR-FREE WORLD!" the protesters chanted. A woman went up to the man at the front.

"Hey!" said Zilla. "It's Ana!" The woman was pointing at Tom and Zilla as she grabbed the megaphone.

"Look!" shouted Ana. "Two kids are brave enough to stand up to the government. This is who we are doing this for. It's our children who will suffer if we keep opening nuclear power stations."

"OK," said Tom. "We've found Ana. Now all we need to do is watch and see what she does."

Chapter 3

The protest went on late into the night. The crowd carried on shouting, and Tom and Zilla joined in. They stood near Ana.

The flames from a bonfire kept them warm. The man with the megaphone told them his name was Alex. He seemed to be the leader.

"It's good to see children supporting the protest," said Alex. "After all, it's you and your friends who will have to live with all the nuclear waste from this power station."

"Yeah, I think nuclear power stations are a bad thing," said Zilla. "But what's the point of waving flags around? Will it change anything?"

Alex laughed. "You sound like Ana! But we can't break into a nuclear power station and stop it working. All we can do is try and get into the news and tell everyone that building nuclear power stations is a bad idea."

Just then, Tom saw that Ana was moving away from the bonfire.

"Back in a bit!" he said, and he followed Ana

as she walked up to the gates of Greyfields.

Then she stopped, with her back to the gates.

She put on a dark hat and gloves, and zipped her black coat right up. Then she bent down to pick up a small rucksack that was hidden in the grass. Tom thought she looked more like a soldier than a protester.

"Trucks!" someone called. It was Alex, speaking through the megaphone. There was a shout from the crowd. Everyone rushed towards the road just as three army trucks pulled up outside the gates. Tom couldn't see Ana any more. The trucks were in the way.

The protesters waved their flags and shouted. The gates to the power station opened and the trucks went through. As the gates closed again, Ana had disappeared.

"She must have got inside the power station!" Tom thought. He ran over to the gates and told the guards what he thought Ana had done.

But nobody would listen. They thought he was just a silly kid.

Tom rushed back to the bonfire to find Zilla. "I need to talk to you!" Tom said and he told her what he had seen.

"What are we going to do?" Zilla asked.

"The guards won't listen," said Tom. "I think we need to tell Marcus and then go in after her. We don't have time to wait for back-up. We don't know what she will do in there!"

They ran to their tent and Tom grabbed bolt-cutters and torches and started packing a small rucksack with other things they might need.

"I'll send a message to Mission Control," said Zilla, tapping at her watch.

"I hope your message gets through," said Tom. "Security probably blocks the phone signal near here so nobody can send secret information about the power station to the wrong people."

"But how will we know?" said Zilla, frowning.

"We just have to hope..." said Tom.

Chapter 4

Tom and Zilla ran up to the metal fence. Tom cut a hole in the fence for them to crawl through. Zilla kept a look-out for the guards.

"Let's go!" said Tom. He was already on the other side of the fence. Zilla crawled through after him.

They ran towards the power station, which was lit up by bright floodlights. They could see the three trucks. Their headlights were still on. When they got close, they lay down on the ground and crawled forward.

They were careful to stay out of the light. Some men were standing around the trucks. They were talking and laughing about the protesters.

"Look!" whispered Tom. He was pointing at someone crawling under one of the trucks.

"It's Ana!" whispered Zilla. "She must have climbed under the truck when it stopped at the gate." Somehow Ana had found a way to hold on underneath as the truck drove in. The men started walking away from the trucks, and Ana crawled out on Tom and Zilla's side. She was wearing headphones.

"What is she doing?" whispered Tom.

They watched as Ana knelt down. She had a tiny torch strapped to her head, which she shone on the ground. She started speaking in Russian.

Suddenly it all made sense. She looked like a soldier. She was speaking in Russian. She was breaking into a nuclear power station. Tom and Zilla looked at one another. They were both thinking the same thing: She's a Russian spy!

They watched Ana feel around for something in the grass, and then pull. It was a manhole cover. She started climbing down into the ground.

"You stay here and tell Mission Control where to find us," Tom whispered. Before Zilla could tell him not to, he began crawling towards the manhole.

He waited a few moments then he climbed down the metal ladder after Ana.

At the bottom, a huge drainpipe led like a tunnel towards the power station buildings. Tom could hear Ana walking carefully through the drainpipe up ahead. He felt in his pocket for his torch but then changed his mind.

If he switched on his torch Ana might see the light. He set off along the drainpipe in the dark. The water came up to his knees. He couldn't see Ana but every now and then he stopped to check that he could still hear her.

Tom began to feel scared. If Ana turned round and saw him he would have nowhere to run. He would be trapped. I shouldn't have come down here by myself, he thought. And then, with a sick feeling in his stomach, Tom realised that he could not hear Ana moving. Where was she?

Chapter 5

Before Tom had time to think, Ana grabbed him by the throat and pulled him to the ground. He kicked out at her but she was too strong.

She pulled a rope from her pocket, tied his hands and feet and pushed him into the stinking water at the bottom of the drainpipe.

She shone her torch into Tom's eyes.

"Where is your sister?" she demanded.

Tom blinked and shook his head.

"If you don't tell me where she is," Ana hissed. "Then when I find her I'm going to really hurt her."

"Well she's not down here!" Tom said. He crossed his fingers, hoping that Zilla had been able to contact Mission Control.

Just then, Tom saw a figure crouching in the shadows behind Ana. Then, the figure leapt forwards and pushed Ana to the ground.

She fell with a splash, and cracked her head on the side of the drainpipe.

Ana tried to get up but the knock to her head had stunned her. Her torch now shone on her attacker's face.

"Zilla!" Tom cried as his sister untied him.

"I heard something banging around in the drain and thought I had better come and save you!" said Zilla, grinning. "Back-up will be here in a minute."

They dragged Ana along the drainpipe. By the time they reached the ladder they could hear that a helicopter had landed above ground.

Two soldiers climbed down. They grabbed Ana and pulled her up out of the drain. Tom and Zilla followed behind.

"Well done, you two!" said one of the soldiers. "Look what we found on her head."

He was holding a small camera.

"She was sending a live video stream to her bosses. Who knows what damage they could have done with information about the power plant. You just helped to catch a Russian spy!"

Bonus Bits!

WHAT ARE NUCLEAR POWER STATIONS?

A nuclear power station is a one where the heat source is a nuclear reactor that uses uranium. The heat is used to generate steam, which drives a steam turbine connected to a generator that produces electricity. Uranium is non-renewable which means that it cannot be replaced once it has all been used up.

WHY ARE SOME PEOPLE AGAINST NUCLEAR POWER?

There are many reasons why people are against nuclear power plants (although there are also a lot of people who think they are a good idea). Here are some of the arguments against them:

money should be spent on using renewable fuels

 old nuclear plants (like Fukushima) can become unsafe and cause a lot of damage to people and surrounding areas

 people might use the technology for weapons instead of simply for power plants.

Do some research into the reasons **for** nuclear power plants. Which side do you agree with?

///// WHAT IS NUCLEAR WASTE? /////

Nuclear waste is what is left over after nuclear fuel has been used in a reactor. People worry about it, as it is 'radioactive' after it has been through the reactor.

QUIZ TIME?

Can you remember what happened in the story? Look back if you need to. There are answers at the end (but no peeking before you finish!)

1. Why are Tom and Zilla needed?

A   they are small enough to slip through the fence

B   their headteacher has sent them

C   they won't be suspected as they are children

D   they know lots about nuclear power stations

2. What did Tim and Zilla's training on maps mean they could do?

A   remember maps

B   read maps

C   join maps together

D   hide maps

3. Who does Ana say they are doing 'it' for?

A   the Russian president

B   children

C   adults

D   the UK president

4. Why do the guards not listen to Tom about Ana?

A   they do not understand him

B   he does not speak their language

C   their helmets go over their ears

D   they think he is a silly kid

5. How did Ana get through the gates?

A   she slipped through the fence

B   she sneaked into the truck

C   she clung on to the bottom of the truck

D   she disguised herself as a guard

6. What did Tom follow Ana into?

A   a metal fence

B   a drainpipe

C   an air vent

D   a tunnel into the building

7. Why could Ana not get up?

A   the water was too deep for her
to stand up in

B   she had broken her leg when she fell

C   her legs were tied together

D   she had knocked her head on
side of drainpipe

WHAT NEXT?

If you enjoyed reading this story and haven't already read Mission Alert: Lab 101, grab yourself a copy and curl up somewhere to read it!

Think about what gadgets might be useful to you if you were a spy. Why not design one on paper – add labels to show what all the parts of it do.

ANSWERS to QUIZ TIME?

1C, 2A, 3B, 4D, 5C, 6B, 7D

Join secret agents Tom and Zilla on their toughest mission yet: a trip to a robotics centre with a dark secret. Can they solve the mysteries of Lab 101?

Join agents Tom and Zilla on another
top-secret spy mission: to investigate an evil
billionaire and a mysterious island.
On Island X, danger is never far away...

Tom and Zilla head to a theme park for their
latest secret spy mission: protecting the son of
a famous scientist from the evil Viper gang. You
never know when the Vipers will attack!

For more high low fiction from Bloomsbury Education visit www.bloomsbury.com